CU00900918

THE DOG'S TALE

Neil C MacArthur

MINERVA PRESS
LONDON
MIAMI   RIO DE JANEIRO   DELHI

THE DOG'S TALE
Copyright © Neil C MacArthur 2001

All Rights Reserved

No part of this book may be reproduced in any form
by photocopying or by any electronic or mechanical means,
including information storage or retrieval systems,
without permission in writing from both the copyright
owner and the publisher of this book.

ISBN 0 75411 590 9

First Published 2001 by
MINERVA PRESS
315–317 Regent Street
London W1R 7YB

Printed in Great Britain for Minerva Press

THE DOG'S TALE

MAP SHOWING ROUTE TAKEN BY LUATH AND TUPPENCE

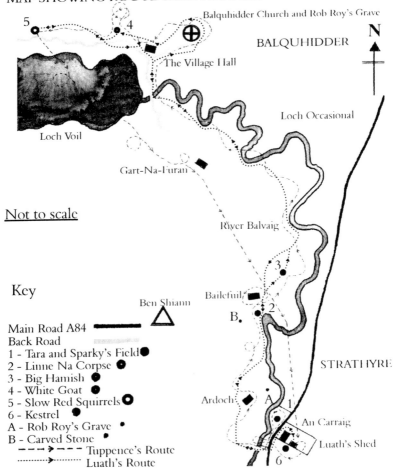

Balquhidder Church and Rob Roy's Grave

BALQUHIDDER

N

The Village Hall

Loch Occasional

Loch Voil

Gart-Na-Furan

Not to scale

River Balvaig

3

Bailefuil

Ben Shiann

Key

2

B.

Main Road A84
Back Road
1 - Tara and Sparky's Field
2 - Linne Na Corpse
3 - Big Hamish
4 - White Goat
5 - Slow Red Squirrels
6 - Kestrel
A - Rob Roy's Grave
B - Carved Stone
→ → → → Tuppence's Route
........→ Luath's Route

STRATHYRE

Ardoch

A

An Carraig

Luath's Shed

6

I have a story for you if you'd care to listen, but before I tell you let me introduce myself. My name is Luath (pronounced Loo-Ah). I am a dog. Well I'm not a dog, I'm a hound – not many people know the difference. I am a deerhound, which doesn't mean I cost a lot of money – although I did – it means I chase deer about all over the place, when I get the chance. That's me at the foot of the page. The handsome devil with the shaggy, blue-grey coat.

The wee bird flying over there is a sparrow. You'll hear more of him later, but I can tell you now he's the strangest passer montanus I've ever met. Oh sorry, tree sparrow.

I don't know whether you have ever seen a deer before, but the best ones to chase are the stags. These are big red animals with branches growing out of their heads. They are more than twice as heavy as me and can run like the wind. But I can catch them. The secret in chasing stags is never do it from the front. These branches called antlers have big jaggy bits on them and if you tackle a big ten or twelve pointer from the front, you're going to end up with a coat full of holes and losing blood at a terrible rate.

I usually give them a start. About fifty yards away I'll bark, which starts them off. Within about a hundred and fifty yards I am upsides with him then I use my shoulder to knock a front leg just as his foot hits the ground. This sends him crashing into the heather, those huge antlers churning up great sods of peat. What I do then is run like the devil in the opposite direction because all I've succeeded in doing is making him really mad. By the time he has untangled himself from the undergrowth I'm clean away looking for the next one. That is what I do for entertainment; it's not everyone's cup of tea but I enjoy it. I must be the fastest hound in the Highlands. Oh, Luath, by the way, means 'swift'.

I live at An Carraig (The Rock), in Strathyre. That's Perthshire. Talking of rocks, that's one thing there are plenty of in the Highlands. Big rocks, little rocks, middle-sized rocks. In fact, you can't move but you fall over a rock. Rocks and water, we've got tons of them both. It's funny, though we are surrounded by rocks, my owner and his daughter go collecting more rocks; they've got standing stones all over the garden. Sometimes I think they're not quite the full five new pence.

Anyway, I'm getting fed up with this nonsense, how about the story? If you can imagine a big wooden shed with a large window on the front left and a big opening on the right, with a small lean-to attached on the right-hand end. The big shed is full of logs, coal, tins of paint, tools, fridges, freezers, a drawing board, hay, saddles, in fact a whole heap of junk. The small lean-to has garden tools round the walls, a desk and a great pile of straw; this is my bed. There is no door on it, it lies open to the elements. I sleep here summer and winter. It can get a bit chilly but I don't mind too much, though one night last winter the temperature went down to minus twenty-two centigrade; I was fine except my ears froze up. That's never happened to me before. Just outside my shed, on the ground, sit two bowls; one for my food and one for my water.

One day I was lying on my bed of straw with my head towards the opening, half dozing, just watching the world go by when a small voice said to me, 'Can I eat out of your dish, Luath?' It was that sparrow, the one I told you about earlier.

'No,' I replied.

'Why not?' asked the bird.

'Go and find your own food like all the other sparrows.'

'But I like your food; it's fantastic!'

'I know, you've

been stealing it when I've been sleeping, haven't you?'

'Yes, but only once or twice. Please, Luath?'

'No, push off little runt.'

'That's not very nice, Luath.'

'I'm not very nice, sparrow, ask the postie. I trapped that female one in the log cabin for about an hour and a half one day, frightened the living daylights out of her.'

'Ooh, go on Luath, please.'

'No.'

'Please.'

'Well, if I did let you…'

'Yes, Luath.'

'If I let you, you would have to do something for me in return!'

'What would that be, Luath?'

'I don't know yet, I'll think about it. Go away and come back later while I give it some thought.'

'Okay, Luath. Thank you. I'll see you later!' The wee bird flew off and I gave the problem long consideration.

What could he do for me? He's only a little bird and sounds a bit dull in the head. I don't think he could manage very much. He couldn't lift or carry anything for me, he's too small. He couldn't tidy the shed up, he's not strong enough. I doubt this is going to work. Actually, I'm surprised he can fly the right way up. I'll just have to tell him I have changed my mind.

When the Sparrow flew back he said, 'What have I to do for you then, Luath?'

'I can't think of anything, Tuppence.'

'That's a nice name, Luath, who are you talking to?'

'To you, Tuppence.'

'Oh, is that my name then, Luath?'

'Yes, Tuppence!'

'Oh, that's just fine. I like that name, thanks Luath. Well, if you can't think of anything I can do for you, maybe I can. Maybe I could lift or carry something for you?'

'No, you are too small.'

'Maybe I could tidy the shed for you?'

'No, Tuppence, you are not strong enough.'

'Maybe I could show you things, Luath?'

'Show me things, what do you mean, Tuppence?'

'I could show you animals and birds and trees and rocks.'

'I think I have seen most of them, Tuppence!'

'There must be something you haven't seen? Have you seen the swans on Loch Lubnaig, Luath?'

'Yes, Tuppence.'

'Have you seen the sleeping lion in Glen Ample, Luath?'

'Yes, Tuppence.'

'Have you seen the rock with the writing on it down the lochside?'

'Yes, Tuppence.'

'Have you seen Tara and Sparky in the field, Luath?'

'Yes, Tuppence, that's just across the road, you stupid bird. Do you not think I get out much?'

'Have you seen the slow red squirrels in

Balquhidder, Luath?'

'Yes, Tuppence. Er no, Tuppence. Mm, I mean I don't know, Tuppence. What did you say, Tuppence?'

'Have you seen the slow red squirrels in Balquhidder, Luath?'

'Oh sorry, Tuppence, for a minute I thought you said, "Have you seen the slow red squirrels in Balquhidder?"'

'I did, Luath.'

'Are you out of your tiny mind, Tuppence?'

'No, Luath, my cousin up the glen told me about them.'

'Why are they slow, Tuppence?'

'I don't know, Luath, maybe they have got bad legs or something. But my cousin told me you don't find them anywhere else in the world, Luath.'

'This cousin of yours, Tuppence…'

'Yes, Luath?'

'Is he as smart as you?'

'Oh no, Luath, he is a lot smarter.'

'He's a lot smarter, Tuppence?'

'Yes, Luath.'

'That slightly worries me, Tuppence.'

'Why, Luath?'

'Oh, I don't know but I have a feeling I am going to find out. All right, Tuppence, if you can show me these slow red squirrels in Balquhidder, you can eat the food out of my dish for ever!'

'Thanks, Luath. We will leave first thing tomorrow morning. It must be five or six miles to the braes. Right, Luath, can I have a bite to eat now?'

'No, Tuppence! Maybe tomorrow night.'

Tuppence flew up into the roof of the big shed, perched there and slept. I spent an uneasy night with my head full of squirrels. I was actually looking forward to our journey but I didn't know why!

Tuppence was up with the lark next day. I took my time; I like my bed. It would be about seven thirty when we left. The route was simple to begin with – out of the garden, across the main road, over the old railway track, heading towards

17

the stone bridge, over the River Balvaig. As we approached the bridge we passed the end of Tara and Sparky's field. Tara and Sparky are Mairi's ponies. Mairi is my owner's daughter; she likes all animals. I can't say I share her feelings. Anyway, Tara is big and gentle and Irish; she is from

Connemara. She has only been here a year or so and she found the winter past a bit cold for her. Sparky is half Welsh, half Shetland, and half daft! She's a trouble-maker. When I am in the field she chases me and tries to nip my bum.

As we passed everything looked normal; that scruffy cat Garry from along the road was lying across Tara's back again, though it never seemed to bother Tara at all. Maybe cats in Connemara sleep on horses' backs. At this point Tuppence took a detour, flew over the ponies' field and came back rather excited.

'What's up, Tuppence?' I asked.

'Do you notice anything different out there this morning, Luath?'

'Can't say I do, Tuppence. That stupid cat is on Tara's back again, but I don't see anything else.'

'That's it, Luath.'

'What do you mean "that's it", Tuppence? Garry is often on Tara's back.'

'I know, Luath, but what time of year is it?'

'It's late spring, Tuppence.'

'What are you on about? Tara was cold in the winter.'

'Yes, I know, Tuppence, spit it out.'

'Tara was shivering during the winter so Mairi put a New Zealand rug on her to keep her warm. Garry would lie on her back in the winter when she had the rug on. The claws, Luath, the claws.'

'Oh no, Tuppence, I see what you mean. In the

winter when Tara moved Garry would sink his claws into the rug to stop himself falling off. Tara doesn't have a rug on. This is going to be fun, Tuppence. I'm going to sit here and watch! Tell me, Tuppence?'

'Yes, Luath?'

'How long do you think it will be before Sparky notices?'

'It will only take as long as it takes me to fly to Sparky's ear.'

The ponies were grazing quietly and moving slowly but when Sparky got the message that changed, and how: Tara was lazy but Sparky could get her moving, and Tara would not have to be moving fast to achieve the desired effect. Sparky gave a couple of little bucks, kicking the air with her hind feet close to Tara's nose and that was it, Tara began to move quicker. And as she moved quicker, Garry's claws began to grip Tara's skin. The faster she moved, the deeper the claws sank in. Tara was trotting now and the look on Garry's face told the story. He had missed the chance of a dignified dismount off this great Irish beast. A trot became a canter, a canter became a gallop. Tara was now in severe pain with Garry's claws sunk in to the hilt. Tara was now in full flight heading straight for the Balvaig. Garry was a nervous wreck but still clung on. As Tara neared the bank of the river she slammed on the anchors, ripping up turf and good grass, and in one movement she turned and reared on her hind legs sending the luckless Garry into the middle of flowing water.

'I've never seen a cat swim before, Tuppence, have you?'

'No, Luath, never.'

'That's just set me up for the day, Tuppence. I enjoyed that!'

'So did I, Luath, so did I.'

From that day on, the hapless cat added the name of another river to his own. He was known ever afterwards as Garry Balvaig.

Time was marching on but we were not. The Garry incident had taken time and we were no more than one hundred yards from my straw. We pushed on over the bridge and took the right fork on the road towards Balquhidder – the left fork takes you to the school and Laggan. We moved passed Ardoch and headed for Bailefuil. We left the road then; it's easier on the feet. It doesn't bother Tuppence. He's up in the air. We proceeded, talking sometimes.

When we left the road Tuppence said, 'Watch out, Luath, there are subtractors in there.'

'What is a subtractor, Tuppence?'

'It's a kind of snake, Luath.'

'Do you not mean adders, Tuppence?'

'No, Luath, I don't think so. I believe they are similar, but shorter, they've had bits taken away. You only find them in Bailefuil.'

'Don't tell me, Tuppence, but your cousin told you this!'

'That's right, Luath, how did you know?'

'Oh, it was only a guess.'

'Do you know what Bailefuil means, Tuppence?'

'I know Baile means a settlement or a village, Luath. Does it mean they couldn't get anyone else in, Luath?'

'Not exactly, Tuppence, it means the settlement of blood.'

'Oh, that sounds a bit nasty, Luath?'

'It was a bit nasty, Tuppence. There was a battle here once, a long time ago.'

'How do you know that, Luath?'

'I've heard the old men talk, Tuppence. They say that there was a dispute between the Buchanans who held territory to the south of here and the MacLarens who had been in Balquhidder for centuries.'

'What was the dispute about, Luath?'

'I don't know but it was more than likely over

land, Tuppence. But apart from that, they quite enjoyed fighting so the reason doesn't really matter.

'Anyway things came to a head and the Buchanan chief led a strong force north through Strathyre to deal with MacLaren and his followers. Now, the MacLarens were a pretty warlike outfit but couldn't raise the numbers that Buchanan could. So he sought an ally and looked no further than that

hardy group of men who had been muscling their way into the top end of Balquhidder for years; the Gregorach. Before the MacGregors agreed to assist, they gained some concessions from the MacLaren chief.'

'What were they, Luath?'

'I don't know them all, Tuppence, but one that sticks in my mind is the fact that, up until then, on the Sabbath, MacGregors had to stand in the church at Balquhidder; but, if they helped in his plight, from that day on they were allowed to sit.'

'That was good of him, Luath!'

'Yes, Tuppence, he obviously had to think long and hard

on that one! Anyway, the battle did not start at Bailefuil; this is where it ended. Buchanan and his men reached the spring waters of Gart-na-Furan, which is a mile or so closer to Balquhidder, expecting to meet an inferior force of MacLarens, which would be easily dealt with.'

'They were in for a bit of a shock, Luath.'

'I think what they saw, Tuppence, would have frightened the life out of them! For standing shoulder to shoulder with the MacLarens were the men who had etched their name on Highland history with the long edge of a broadsword. Clan Labhran and Clan Gregor fell on Buchanan like a thunderbolt from above. Buchanan desperately tried to retreat but they were overtaken and slaughtered at Bailefuil. Some would escape to tell the story, Tuppence, but a good number didn't. Do you see that bend in the river there? That's Linne-na-Corpse – the pool of bodies. The dead Buchanans would have been stripped of weapons and clothing and their naked bodies would have been dumped in the river.'

'How many were killed, Luath?'

'I'm not sure, Tuppence, but there is a stone just up the hill there, beside the back road which has carved on it the number fifty-five and the image of a broadsword.'

'Let's move on, Luath, the feathers on the back of my neck are sticking up.'

Our pace had slowed with all this talk of battles, as we followed the bends in the river along the flood plain. Animals graze here in the summer, and fish in the winter. This bit is known as Loch Occasional. I jumped another dyke approaching Gart-na-Furan, a pleasant field with cattle grazing, which I strolled through. The sun was now high in the sky and I was enjoying the company of the little sparrow.

That is until I strolled past a cow that wasn't a cow. Tuppence was twittering something from above, but I couldn't hear. Passing this cow, I realised it had straight horns and all the other cows had curved horns. I had just passed it when I heard an almighty roar. I turned my head to the

rear only to see the enormous beast snorting fire
and ripping up the turf with a huge cloven hoof.
That's not a cow, I thought, that's big Hamish the
bull; why does he not have a ring in his nose?
Because nobody has got close enough to put one
in, I feared. Now, I'm fast, but over thirty yards
Hamish is Olympic standard. Luckily for me the
dyke at the other end of the field was close but it
was within five seconds of
being a pile

of stones again.

He lunged at me like the whole of Clan Gregor en masse. I burst my lungs to escape, leaped and cleared the dyke; Hamish went through it, huge stones filling the air like confetti. I was safe; well, half a mile later I checked the situation, and was safe. Hamish had a headache. Now where was that stupid bird?

'Tuppence, where are you?'

'I'm here, Luath. Sorry, Luath, I tried to warn you.'

'What were you twittering about, Tuppence?'

'Well, a couple of years ago someone called Jack Russel had bitten

big Hamish's ankles and he doesn't like dogs any more.'

'I'm not a dog, Tuppence, I'm a hound.'

'I don't think Hamish knows the difference, Luath.'

'I like chasing beasts but I don't like being the quarry.'

We moved on. We had a clear view of Balquhidder now as we followed the river again.

Tuppence and I didn't speak much for a while. Then he came out with a beauty.

'Do you know that woman, Luath?'

'What woman, Tuppence?'

'That woman.'

'Tuppence, who do you mean?'

'She's got a face like a pig and swears a lot.'

'Yes, I know her.'

'Well, she keeps her shoes and her knitting in a portable toilet. The one they use for the caravan.'

'What about it, Tuppence?'

'Oh, nothing, Luath, I just thought you would like to know.'

'That's going to be handy, Tuppence. When I'm deep in conversation with Donald MacLaren of MacLaren about politics, I can just throw that one in!'

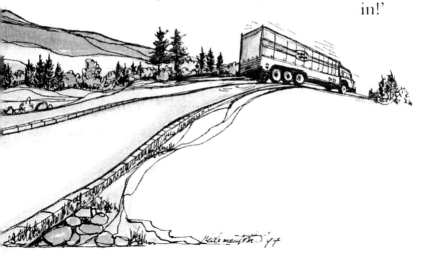

'Yes, Luath. I thought it would be useful.'

As we moved on to Balquhidder I said to Tuppence, 'What would you like to be if you weren't a sparrow?'

'Oh, that's an easy one, Luath, I'd like to be fast over the ground like you.'

'Why's that, Tuppence?'

'Well, I can fly about up in the air, upside down, loop the loop, all that stuff, but on the ground all I can do is hop about. Remember the day you were chasing lorries instead of deer?'

'Yes, Tuppence, I remember.'

'Well, you came out of the car park just south of Strathyre like a rocket with one of them in your sights. They're big those trucks, aren't they?'

'Yes, about fifty feet long.'

'Well, you chased it all the way through the village to Creagan just outside the thirty limit.'

'Yes, I know, Tuppence, I was there. Well, what's the point?'

'Ah, yes, Luath, what amazed me about that was you came out the car park at exactly five o'clock, and you were moving so fast that when you reached Creagan it was just five minutes to five. You didn't catch it though did you, Luath?'

'No, Tuppence, it was moving faster than me. It was your cousin wasn't it, Tuppence?'

'What about my cousin, Luath?'

'It was him, Tuppence, wasn't it?'

'Wasn't it what, Luath?'

'He told you how to tell the time, didn't he?'

'Oh that. Yes, Luath, of course.'

'Thought so.'

We passed Gart-na-Furan and a short time later crossed the river again just south of Loch Voil and headed straight for the village hall.

'We should go left here, Luath, the squirrels are along the Loch side about a mile from here.'

'Right, Tuppence, but before we do that let's go and have a look at the church. It's only a few hundred yards out of our way.'

'Okay, Luath. Isn't that where Rob Roy is buried, Luath?'

'Well, yes and no, Tuppence.'

'What do you mean, yes and no? He is either buried there or not.'

'All the tourists come here to look at his grave, Tuppence, but he is not actually buried here.'

'Where is he buried then, Luath?'

'Shush, keep your voice down, I don't want

everyone to hear.'

'All right Luath, where is he buried then?'

'He is buried at Ardoch.'

'*Ardoch!*'

'Keep your voice down, Tuppence.'

'Who told you this, Luath? I don't believe you, everyone knows Rob Roy is buried in front of the old church in Balquhidder.'

'Well, if you don't believe me I won't tell you the

story. Let's go and look for these stupid squirrels, come on.'

'Why don't you tell me the story anyway, Luath.'

'No.'

'Go on, Luath, tell me.'

'*No*!'

'Please.'

'No, it's too scary for a silly sparrow.'

'No, it won't be, Luath.'

'If the feathers on the back of your neck were sticking out at Bailefuil, you'll not be able to handle this one, bird.'

'If I get too scared, Luath, I will just fly away. Who told you the story anyway?'

'The old hag on Ben Shiann.'

'I didn't know there was an old hag on Ben Shiann, Luath.'

'No, you wouldn't, Tuppence. You fly around backwards, upside down with your eyes shut and your feet stuck up your bottom!'

'That sounds quite difficult, Luath! I'll have to

try that! Who is the old hag, Luath?'

'She's one of the Shiann, Tuppence.'

'I don't believe in fairies, Luath.'

'She's not a fairy. Fairies are stupid, wee things with wings sticking out of their backs, a bit like sparrows, and they only inhabit children's books. The Shiann are the small folk, the little people, the same as in Ireland; fully grown they are about the height of a ten-year-old boy. They often wear green clothing.'

'I don't believe you, Luath.'

'You don't believe very much, Tuppence, but you seem to believe in these slow red squirrels, eh?'

'Yes, my cousin told me.'

'Do you think I will get a chance to meet this cousin of yours?'

'I hope so, Luath!'

'So do I, Tuppence, so do I!'

'I've flown over Ben Shiann often and never seen her.'

'She lives inside the hill, you know the sticky

out bit at the top, the plug of the extinct volcano…'

'I didn't know Ben Shiann used to be a volcano,
Luath.'

'That doesn't surprise me, Tuppence, why don't
you check that one out with your cousin?'

'I will, I will. Octolostabit, Luath.'

'Octo what, Tuppence?'

'Octolostabit, Luath.'

'In heaven's name what does Octolostabit
mean, Tuppence?'

'I thought you'd know that one, Luath.'

'Well, I don't. What does it mean?'

'It means that's the eighth time today I didn't
know where I was.'

'I'm not even going to ask, Tuppence; I am
going to try and ignore that one, if I can.
Well anyway, there is a maze of passageways and
chambers under the top of that hill, she lives in
there. Have you seen the lines of light at the top
in the darkness?'

'Yes, I have, Luath, what are they?'

'That's the light from the fires, Tuppence; you sometimes see them through the cracks in the rocks.'

'What are the fires for, Luath?'

'Just to keep her warm, Tuppence. Oh, and something else…'

'What else, Luath, what else?'

'It doesn't matter, Tuppence, forget it.'

'No, Luath, tell me.'

'She roasts sparrows on them!'

'*She what*! I'm never going near that hill again, Luath, never, never, never.'

'Just a little joke, Tuppence!'

'Goodness, Luath, you nearly frightened the feathers off me. How old is she, Luath?'

'She's getting on a bit now, Tuppence, she was born in 1671, so that makes her 326.'

'Don't be ridiculous, Luath, human beings don't last that long.'

'She's not human, Tuppence, she's not human. You can spend the night in that hill and when you come out in the morning, it's a year later.'

'Maybe you should forget the story, Luath. Let's head for the squirrels.'

'No, Tuppence, you wanted to hear, now you're going to listen. After Rob Roy died, two coffins left the house for burial…'

'Why was that, Luath?'

'I think just to confuse people, Tuppence, because even in death Red Robert MacGregor had many enemies. News travelled fast in the hills, as it still does, and news of Rob's death eventually reached the cities of Perth, Dundee, Aberdeen, Glasgow and Edinburgh. It was listened to with keen interest by a group of young medical students at the University of Edinburgh. They were always on the lookout for bodies to cut up.'

'Stop it, Luath, you are just making this up as

you go along. Who in their right mind would want to cut up bodies, Luath?'

'This was the time of the body snatchers, Tuppence. Bodies fetched a good price in the cities, people were keen to learn more about the human body and how it worked; it's called medical research.'

'Well, I think it's disgusting, Luath, they didn't do it to sparrows, did they?'

'Your scrawny little body wouldn't fetch very much would it, Tuppence?'

'No, I don't suppose it would.'

'Anyway, they'd have to pluck you before they could cut you up!'

'Don't, Luath, that's horrible.'

'Anyway, these students devised a plan to snatch the body of Rob Roy MacGregor and take it back to Edinburgh to chop it up.'

'Well, that's just plain stupid. Why would they do that? Apart from being dangerous with all these wild Highland men about, there must have been more bodies in Edinburgh to steal than

Balquhidder.'

'Well, that's true, Tuppence, but Rob Roy was a very famous man and physically a fine specimen, robust and powerful, and there is a story that he had unusually long arms. They even said he could tie the garters on his kilt hose without bending down. But the old hag said that was a bit of a joke. You know how these Campbells like a laugh.'

'I thought Rob's mother was a Campbell, Luath?'

'She was, Tuppence, but I bet she laughed too.'

'Anyway, these students wanted to cut up Rob's body to see what made him tick.'

'Did he tick?'

'No, you dozy bird, it's an expression.'

'I don't know much about expressions, Luath. I've only got one; it's difficult to change it with a beak.'

'Oh no, Tuppence, just shut up and listen. The students planned their trip to arrive in Balquhidder at the dead of night…'

'That's a good one, Luath, the dead of night, eh!'

'Dry up would you. They had obviously planned the operation quite well...'

'That's another good one!'

'Shut up, twit! Because when they reached Balquhidder they had changed into Highland garb, and even had a few words in Gaelic in case they were challenged at any point...'

'You mean if anyone stopped them they would say *a few words in Gaelic*, Luath?'

'Yes, Tuppence.'

'So if they were stopped they would all say *a few words in Gaelic*?'

'*Yes*, Tuppence,

what about it?'

'How do you say *a few words in Gaelic*, in Gaelic, Luath? Or did they use English?'

'I have a few words in Gaelic for you Tuppence, but unfortunately I can't use them here. Do you understand, Tuppence?'

'Yes, Luath. I think I know the words you mean. I'm surprised at you, Luath, I didn't think you knew words like that!'

'Can I go on now, Tuppence?'

'Yes, please, Luath, it isn't really all that scary now. Is it?'

'I think that might have something to do with you, Tuppence! They exhumed the body quietly, left the grave as they had found it and got clean away back to Edinburgh without anyone in the parish of Balquhidder suspecting anything...'

'They wouldn't be very clean after digging up a... sorry, Luath.'

'Tuppence can you fly without tail feathers?'

'Don't know, Luath, never tried.'

'We'll try it later Tuppence, okay?'

'Okay, Luath.'

'Well, the students examined Rob's body. What they found out I don't know but when they were finished they sewed it up again and decided to do the Christian thing and take it back to Balquhidder for reburial.'

'Was Rob Roy a Christian then, Luath?'

'Yes, Tuppence, what did you think he was?'

'I thought he was a MacGregor.'

'For you, that's quite amusing, Tuppence.'

'Thanks, Luath.'

'The return trip didn't quite go according to plan…'

'You mean these apprentice surgeons made a bit of a mess of the operation.'

'*Yes*, Tuppence, good one. I am kind of getting the hang of your sense of humour, my head is slightly numb though. The MacGregors in Balquhidder knew of their approach…'

'How did they know that, Luath?'

'I'm not sure, Tuppence, but it's possible there were one or two MacGregors at the university…'

'Were they quite brainy the MacGregors?'

'Yes, they were, Tuppence, and proved that time and time again over the following years. They would possibly get wind of what was happening in the mortuary at the medical department and inform the people back home. Anyway, they knew they were coming and the MacGregors started streaming out of Balquhidder like a winter torrent, heading south along the route we took today. Luckily for the

students they too were warned of the MacGregors' approach at Ardoch. Remember Ardoch, the big white house we passed this morning?'

'Yes, Luath, opposite Tara and Sparky's field. Who would warn them, Luath?'

'Oh, probably a Buchanan in Strathyre, Tuppence. Remember Bailefuil?'

'Oh, yes, what happened then?'

'They quickly found a secluded spot in the beech wood near

Ardoch Lodge, interred Rob's body there, then removed themselves out of the Strath in jig time.'

'What's jig time, Luath?'

'It means quickly like the dance.'

'I didn't know a jig was a dance, Luath.'

'Well, maybe not, sparrows don't do a lot of dancing do they, Tuppence?'

'No, Luath, a bit of hopping but no dancing.'

'Anyway, they got clean away again. Don't say it. They went back to their lodging in Edinburgh to hope for obscurity.'

'Why didn't the MacGregors catch them, Luath?'

'Well they would only pursue them to the pass of Leny, Tuppence.'

'Why's that?'

'You're not very smart are you, Tuppence?'

'No, Luath. But why?'

'The pass of Leny is where you leave the Highlands and enter the Lowlands, and 150 wild Highlanders marauding into the Lowlands with murder on their minds would have the whole of

Scotland in uproar and there would be more reprisals against Clan Gregor.'

'Had they been dealt with harshly before then, Luath?'

'You know, Tuppence, sometimes I think there is a brain in that tiny little cranium of yours. You know at one time you couldn't even call yourself MacGregor. Rob Roy himself was known as Robert Campbell for a while. Just let's say they weren't very popular with the authorities.'

'Do you think they would ever ban the name Tuppence, Luath?'

'I don't think so.'

'Who called me Tuppence anyway?'

'I did, Tuppence. That was just yesterday; have you forgotten already?'

'Why did you call me Tuppence?'

'Well, I didn't think you were worth it.'

'I don't understand, Luath, what does Tuppence mean anyway?'

'It means two pennies.'

'Oh good, that means I am quite valuable then.'

'Yes, Tuppence.'

'Is that the end of the story, Luath?'

'Well, not exactly, Tuppence, there is another part, but nobody knows this bit, just the old hag and me. Are you sure you want to hear it? Time's getting on and we haven't seen the squirrels yet.'

'What time it is anyway, Luath?'

'It's two o'clock, Tuppence.'

'Things are dragging a bit today, Luath, aren't they?'

'What do you mean, Tuppence?'

'Well, this time yesterday it was four o'clock.'

'Tuppence…'

'Yes, Luath.'

'Never mind, Tuppence, we'll just have to work at it.'

'Right, Luath.'

'I don't know

how the old hag knew this part of the story but a lot of these old craturs have the sight, don't they, Tuppence?'

'I've got sight, Luath, there's nothing usual about that, is there?'

'No, you dope, I mean the second sight.'

'Does that mean you see things very quickly, like in a second?'

'No, no, no, Tuppence. It means you can see into the future and into the past and into the minds of animals and people; you can tell what's happening to someone even if they are on the other side of the world…'

'I didn't know the world had sides, Luath. I thought it was spherical.'

'Oh, you thought it was spherical, did you, Tuppence. Well you're right, it is spherical. It's another one of those expressions. I've actually got a touch of the second sight myself, Tuppence. I can tell when my tea's ready…'

'How do you know that, Luath?'

'Well, it's usually about five o'clock.'

'That's impressive, Luath. Come on, Luath, what is the other bit of the story?'

'Well, Tuppence, it goes like this. The students reached Edinburgh safely, unobserved and into their lodgings, thinking they had been very fortunate to do so. They knew the Gregorach would not leave the high country en masse. But for one of them at least, the problems started...'

'What problems, Luath?'

'Well, he was suffering from stress...'

'Stress, what's stress, Luath?'

'Stress, Tuppence, is one of those things you never suffer from until some idiot tells you what the word means.'

'Don't tell me, Luath. How does this old hag know all this, Luath?'

'I told you, Tuppence, she was there. I told you what age she was. She knew Rob Roy MacGregor, they used to meet at the little house at the foot of Ben Shiann, close by Ardoch. It's still there Tuppence, we passed by it this morning. She still has the knife, Tuppence; I have seen it. A little knife with a fine black handle. Rob carried it everywhere under his left armpit, Tuppence. Tuppence? Where are you Tuppence?'

'I'm up here, Luath, at the top of this big larch.'

'What are you doing up there?'

'I was getting a bit scared, Luath. I had to fly away.'

'I'm not finished the story yet, Tuppence. Come down.'

'No, keep going Luath, but if I can listen from a distance it'll not seem so bad.'

'I don't want to shout, Tuppence. I can't let anyone hear this; I promised.'

'You promised who, Luath?'

'The old hag, Tuppence.'

'What will she do if she finds out, Luath?'

'I don't know, Tuppence, I don't know.'

'Are you scared, Luath?'

'Yes, Tuppence, I'm scared, but stories must be told. If stories are not told and music is not played our lives will become as empty as these hills.'

'But she told you, Luath.'

'Yes, Tuppence, but I sleep by her feet sometimes while she sews.'

'Oh, I didn't know, Luath. I would like to hear the rest of the story.'

'Are you sure, Tuppence, are you sure?'

'Yes, I'm sure.'

'This student, I don't know his name but it was probably Jimmy…'

'Why would it be Jimmy, Luath?'

'I'm not sure, Tuppence, but nearly every male in Glasgow is called Jimmy and the females are called Hen.'

'But I thought he came from Edinburgh?'

'Yes, he did Tuppence, but Jimmy is good enough for him. Anyway, they all look the same to me. Since his return from Ardoch he didn't sleep well. At night he saw MacGregors in every shadow, saw blood in every puddle and, when he closed his eyes, saw hundreds of howling, distorted faces coming out of the darkness, moonlight glinting on whistling broad, blue, fluted blades…'

'He had a vivid imagination, didn't he, Luath?'

'Yes, he did, Tuppence, and he had only ever seen one MacGregor in his life and he was lying dead on a marble slab. If you know Edinburgh you'll know that at this time it was a dirty, stinking city. With no sanitation, the citizens hurled their sewage out of the windows of their tall buildings into the street, with little regard to passers by, only a shout of Gardy-Loo…'

'What did that mean, Luath?'

'It's just corrupted French, Tuppence. I think it means watch out for the water. Most of the buildings were clustered about the castle and its tail down to Holyrood Palace. The first skyscrapers in the world, Tuppence. Some of them fifteen stories high…'

'Is that why they call it the High Street, Luath?'

'No, I don't think so, Tuppence, but that's a better story. Get it? "Better story", Tuppence, as in fifteen stories?'

'Sorry, Luath, missed that one; it went over my head.'

'Tuppence?'

'Yes, Luath.'

'Shut up.'

'No, Luath.'

'Okay, Tuppence. This was Jimmy's environment. The university was a grim collection of buildings not far from the High Street, where he lodged. He spent his days going back and forward to his studies, winding his way through the dreary closes of Edinburgh and he spent his nights in fear…'

'What are closes, Luath?'

'They are just little streets that connect the bigger streets together. His studies would push the frontiers of medical science ever forward, but he and his colleagues had violated one of the most sacred graves in the Highlands and he knew it. To the Lowlander, Rob Roy MacGregor was an outlaw, a thief, a rogue, a Jacobite, a heathen and a scoundrel; to the Highlander he was all these things and more. He spoke Gaelic, English, Lowland Scots and understood Latin and French. He was the captain of Clan Gregor, not its chief but its protector. The leader in battle and mentor of the young chief to be. He also invented "blackmail" and was one of the finest swordsmen in the Highlands. So, as you can see, Tuppence, he wasn't Mr Popular with everyone…'

'He was a terrible man, wasn't he, Luath?'

'He certainly was, Tuppence, a terrible man! However, the weeks were going by and Jimmy's dreams were diminishing; he could

sleep now and the gruesome images were fading. He began to feel more like he felt pre-Ardoch. He could laugh now and his studies were progressing well. He was proving to be one of the better students in his class. In fact, his results in anatomy were the best in the university. The professor was pleased with him.'

'That's good, isn't it, Luath, I'm glad he was doing well.'

'Yes, Tuppence, so was I! One night he was out with his friends – the very students that were with him at Ardoch; there were five in all – drinking in one of the hostelries in the Lawn Market. The drinks flowed and the tongues became looser; they recounted incidents from their journey north. They had a grand evening, but lessons were early in the morning and it was past midnight, they would have to go back to their lodgings. As the other four left the hostelry, Jimmy shouted to them that he would catch them up in a couple of minutes; he was engrossed with a young serving girl. He left a few minutes after them waving cheerily goodbye to the girl. He was slightly the worse for drink and swayed gingerly on his way. He followed the route his friends had taken, through a claustrophobic close. I'm not going to tell you what claustrophobic means, Tuppence, look it up in the dictionary…'

'What does dictionary mean, Luath?'

'He had gone but a few yards into the close when he noticed something on the ground ahead of him. It was dark and his eyes had not adjusted yet to the conditions. The whisky didn't help. As he got closer he saw that it was a plaid, a tartan plaid of a red hue. But there were shapes below it. He staggered towards it and, bending slowly, he pulled it back, all the way back. Fear gripped him like a vice. Four bodies, placed neatly side by side, eyes staring, colour gone – his friends, *his friends*. Then a hand, a hard Highland hand, clamped nostrils and mouth shut, capturing the final breath. Then soft Gaelic whispered unknown words of venom in an ear that would hear no more. Then, between ribs number six and seven, Ferara's finest blade plunged through vital organs; then the flood and the pain. Then the little knife with the fine black handle, graloched like a stag on an empty highland moor. Then later, much later, she came, the red one, the vixen with her cubs, and in the morning an empty shell and the cobbles licked clean. All around. Tuppence, that was the final anatomy lesson for Jimmy. Tuppence? Tuppence, where are you?'

'Sorry, Luath, fell out the sky. Och, it wasn't that scary, I can handle that. I hope that's the end now, Luath?'

'Yes, Tuppence, that's the end of that one. Come on, we haven't seen these squirrels yet.'

'Right, Luath. Let's go, not far now.

Straight past the village
hall, Luath.'
    'Okay, Tuppence.'
    We were now going
through a field with a
gentle slope running down
towards Loch Voil, there
was a white goat grazing
        there at the top of
            the field.

Tuppence was flying quite high when he whistled and shouted, 'Luath.'

'What is it Tuppence?'

'Look over there, Luath, at the bottom end of the field.'

We both went over.

'What is it, Tuppence?'
'It looks like a hole in the ground, Luath, and it's deep.'
As we got closer we realised it was very deep.

'I'll fly down and see how deep it is, Luath.'

'I wouldn't if I were you, Tuppence, you don't know what's down there.'

'All right, Luath, but how can we find out how deep it is?'

'Drop a stone down and wait for a sound of it hitting the bottom.'

Tuppence picked up a wee stone in his beak and dropped it down the hole. We waited for the sound of it hitting the bottom but no sound was heard.

'Drop a bigger one down, Luath.'

I pushed a large stone that was sitting near the edge into the hole. Again we waited, but no sound.

'It really is deep, Luath. Look, Luath, there's a big log. Let's roll that into the hole; we must hear something from that.'

I put my shoulder to the big log and rolled it nearer to the hole. 'You're not much help, Tuppence, are you?'

'Well, it's too big for me, Luath.'

Eventually, I had the big log beside the hole and pushed it in.

'Listen hard this time, Tuppence.'

'Yes, Luath.'

'I still don't hear anything, Tuppence, do you?'

'No, Luath, nothing, except for something behind.'

We looked around and that white goat that was grazing peacefully at the top of the field was now charging straight towards us. It looked really angry and its hoofs sounded like a cavalry charge.

'Oh no! Big Hamish all over again, only this time I don't think I can outrun him; he's moving too fast.'

At the last moment Tuppence flew straight up and I dived to the side. The goat went straight past us and dived straight down the big hole. Just then we heard a man's voice shouting to us.

'I say, chaps, you haven't seen a white goat around here anywhere, have you?'

'Funnily enough,' I said, 'we have. A white goat just charged across the field and dived straight down that big hole over there.'

The man thought for a minute, then said, 'It's all right chaps, that can't be my goat. My goat was tied to a big log,' and then walked away. Tuppence fell out the sky again, this time in an agony of laughter. I fell over myself, ribs aching. It took us quite a time to recover our composure.

'English,' I said to Tuppence later.

'Was he English, Luath, how do you know that?'

'Funny accent, Tuppence.'

'Are all people around here with funny accents English?'

'Most of them, Tuppence.'

'Where are the other ones from?'

'Falkirk, I think. I am sure he is the one that stopped the local boys playing shinty at the end of the Loch, Tuppence.'

'Is that right, Luath. Well, I'm glad he lost his goat.'

'Do you not think he is missing a few marbles as well, Tuppence?'

'Yes, Luath. Come on, not far now.'

We were moving along the lochside near the road that takes you to Tulloch, Craigruie and Inverlochlaraig, where Rob Roy once farmed, when we heard twittering voices.

'What's that, Tuppence?'

'That's my relatives, Luath.'

We approached a tree by the roadside and on a branch was a row of little tree sparrows. They were all on top of the branch, except for one who was upside down.

'Is that your cousin there, Tuppence?'

'Yes, Luath, how did you know?'

'Just a wild guess, Tuppence, just a wild guess. Hold it a second, Tuppence, hold it.'

'What Luath?'

'What's that on the trunk of the tree, Tuppence?'

'It's a white board, Luath.'

'I can see it's a white board, but what does it say on the white board?'

I don't think it says anything, Luath. Boards

can't speak.'

'*No*, Tuppence. All right, what is written on the board?'

'I don't know, Luath, I can't read English.'

'I suppose you can only read sparrow!'

'No, Luath, I can't read at all.'

'Will I read it to you, Tuppence?'

'Yes please, Luath.'

'Are you quite prepared for this Tuppence?'

'Oh yes, Luath, ready.'

'SLOW! Exclamation mark. RED SQUIRRELS ON ROAD.'

'Oh, that's a bit of a downer, Luath. Still never mind, no harm done.'

'No harm done, you clot! I've nearly been

steamrolled by a big hairy
bull and nearly skewered
on the horns of an
angry goat, and you say
no harm done.'

'They were both
nearlys though,

SLOW!
RED SQUIRRELS
ON ROAD

Luath, weren't they?'

'Yes, Tuppence, you're right. I'm not angry, I've had worse days than this. Anyway I'm heading home now, Tuppence.'

'I'll stay with my cousin for a while, Luath. I'll see you back in Strathyre later.'

'Check with your cousin, Tuppence, there might be something else we can search for another day!'

'Right, Luath, I'm sure there will be.'

'So am I, Tuppence, so am I.'

And with that, I headed home alone, retracing my steps but avoiding one big deep hole in the ground and giving a wide berth to a certain big hairy bull.

I got back to my shed and my meal inside the hour; I ate heartily and drank deeply, remembering to leave some for Tuppence. I settled on the straw and slept. I was quite tired.

A couple of hours later I was suddenly awakened by a piercing scream coming out of the north. It was in the distance but was getting nearer. I leapt out of bed and stood listening intently. As the sound got closer I thought I recognised the voice but wasn't sure, then it dawned on me it was Tuppence. Tuppence has quite a deep voice for a sparrow but at the moment he was screaming like a banshee. A few seconds later he came into sight, skirting the side of the log cabin and flying low over the standing stones.

'Oh my god, Tuppence!'

This was serious for on his tail was the biggest, angriest, most belligerent kestrel I'd ever seen. If he had been any closer to Tuppence he would have been in front of him. As they crossed over the garden dodging birch and rowan, I jumped as high as I could, eager to snap that falcon's back, but I had no chance. Tuppence was on his own in this one. I put up a quick silent prayer to the Celtic gods of war to assist the wee bird. He certainly needed it; I was a mere spectator.

Tuppence, still screaming, headed for the rear of my shed; it looked to me as if all was lost. I prepared myself for the sight of blood and feathers cascading down from the sky. He was going past the tree on the right-hand side, then banked steeply to the left. He made a complete circuit of the tree about three quarters of the way up, but the big kestrel was still on his tail, curved beak snapping at tail feathers. Tuppence completed another circuit; same result. That big raptor could smell blood now and, as they came round for the third time, Tuppence was silent, and the kestrel's call of 'kee-kee-kee' signalled the final act. At this precise moment Tuppence dived straight into the heart of the tree followed immediately by the falcon. That was it, I thought. There was the most almighty stramash in the branches, sickening sounds of heavy blows being struck, dull thuds like the sound of broadsword hitting targe, screaming. It was a terrible melee with me standing helpless at the foot of the tree. My little friend of a day, my little warrior gone to Valhalla.

Not a bit of it. The kestrel's body was thrown out of the tree backwards, hit the ground with a thud. There he was lying on his back, eyes closed,

beak open, wings outstretched and feet up in the air.

A second later, out flew Tuppence, twittering happily. As he flew down to me I shouted, 'Claymore! Tuppence Claymore! That was a hell of a battle Tuppence, how did you manage that.'

'Oh, it was nothing at all, Luath, no problem whatsoever.'

'And you without a weapon to hand, Tuppence, not a weapon in sight.'

'Well, Luath, not strictly true.'

'What do you mean, Tuppence? What do you mean?'

'Look up at the tree, Luath, look up at the tree.'

As I looked up I saw a branch dip slowly, and out of the heart of the tree appeared that enormous ginger tom cat that lives over the dyke. He was heading down to the ground to finish off the kestrel.

'How did you know he was in there, Tuppence?'

'Well, I didn't really, Luath, but once or twice before I've seen him in there waiting for careless little birds. On the first circuit I saw him, and I thought I would take him in a bigger meal. I just sat on a branch inside the tree above them and watched. He's got a marvellous right cross, that cat you know!'

'You flew into the gates of Hell and flew out again, Tuppence.'

'Yes, Luath, isn't it great.'

Before ginger tom had reached the ground, the kestrel had come around. He had only been knocked out, and he didn't waste any time getting out of the garden. And do you know something, we have never seen that kestrel again.

'Have we Tuppence?'

'No, Luath, never.'

'Come and get something to eat Tuppence, you deserve it.'

We talked till quite late then Tuppence said, 'I hear the pipes, Luath.'

'Yes, I hear them too, Tuppence. I'll have to go.'

'It sounds like they are coming from Ben Shiann, Luath.'

'Yes, Tuppence. Look after the place for me.'

'Can I come, Luath?'

'Not this time, friend. See you tomorrow.'

'Luath, Luath, what tune is he playing? What's the name of the tune?'

'MacGregors Gathering, Tuppence,
MacGregors Gathering…'